This Walker book belongs to:

_____

_____

_____

For Alice Mary Hathway – J.W.

For Paul and Denise – J.F.

First published 2008 by Walker Books Ltd, 87 Vauxhall Walk, London SE11 5HJ

This edition published 2009

2 4 6 8 10 9 7 5 3

Text © 2008 Jeanne Willis

Illustrations © 2008 Jan Fearnley

The right of Jeanne Willis and Jan Fearnley to be identified as author and illustrator respectively of this work has been asserted by them in accordance with the Copyright, Designs and Patents Act 1988

This book has been typeset in Stempel Schneider

Printed in China

British Library Cataloguing in Publication Data: a catalogue record for this book is available from the British Library

ISBN 978-1-4063-1765-7

www.walker.co.uk

Mummy Do You Love Me?

JEANNE WILLIS   JAN FEARNLEY

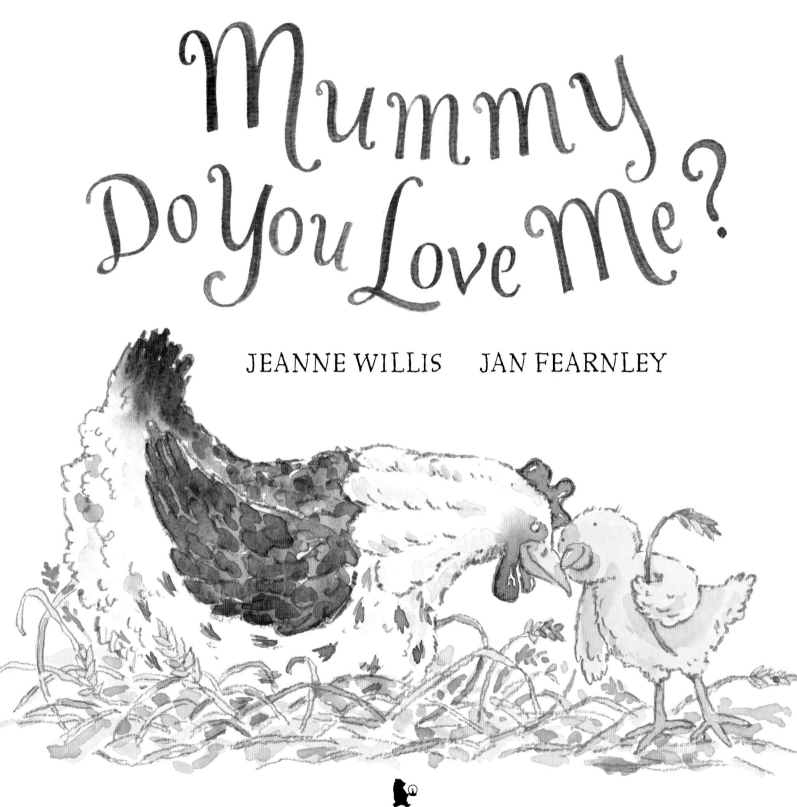

WALKER BOOKS

AND SUBSIDIARIES

LONDON • BOSTON • SYDNEY • AUCKLAND

"Mummy, do you love me?"
asked Little Chick.

"I love you more than words can
ever say," said his mummy.

And she gave him a peck
on the cheek.

"But will you *always* love me,
even if I look like this?" he cheeped.
And he pulled a funny face.
"Yes!" she said. "You'll *always*
be beautiful to me."

Just to make sure, Little Chick
found the muddiest puddle
on the farm.

And **jumped** in it.

When he came back, he was
covered from head to tail in muck.
"Mummy," he said, "do you *still* love me,
even now I'm muddy?"

"Yes," she said. "You're *still* my sweet Little Chick underneath."

And she made him all fluffy again.

Just then, his friends called round.
They had a race.

Little Chick didn't win.

"Mummy," he said, "do you *still* love me,
even though I came last?"
"Yes," said his mummy. "You *always*
come first with me."

And she gave him a red rose.
Little Chick ran to show his friends.
"Your mummy must *really* love you!"
they said.

But on
the way
home

he dropped the rose …

and
all
the
petals
fell
off.

"Mummy," he cheeped, "do you *still* love me,
even though I ruined my rose?"
"Yes," she said. "Roses don't last, but
my love for you will last for ever."

And she put her wing around him.

Little Chick was so happy to be loved,
he cheeped and he chirped
and he crowed ...

very, very loudly.

"Please be quiet,"
said his mummy.

But Little Chick
wouldn't.

He shrieked and screeched
and squawked even
louder.

His mummy tried again.
"*Please* be quiet,
Little Chick."

But Little Chick wouldn't listen. He just kept shouting

louder

and

louder.

So his mummy shouted back...

BE QUIET, LITTLE CHICK!

Little Chick
couldn't believe his ears:
his mummy had shouted at him!

Didn't she love him any more?

He was so upset, he ran away and hid
his head under his wing.

His mummy came to look for him.
"What's wrong, Little Chick?" she said.
"Mummy," he cried, "do you *still* love
me, even when I'm bad?"
"Little Chick," she said, "sometimes you
make me mad, sometimes you make me
sad, but no matter what you say
or do, I will *always* love you."

"Why?" asked Little Chick.
"Because I'm your mummy,"
she said.

"I love you too," he said.

"Ah," said his mummy. "But will you *always* love me, even if I look like this?" And she pulled a funny face.

Little Chick laughed and laughed.
"Mummy," he said, "sometimes you make
me mad, sometimes you make me sad,
but no matter what you say or do,
I will *always* love you."

"Why?" asked his mummy.

"Because I'm your Little Chick!"
he said.

Other books by Jeanne Willis

978-0-7445-9650-2

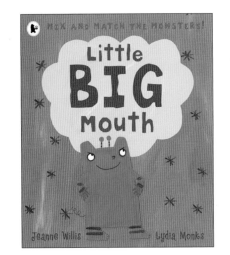

978-1-4063-1239-3

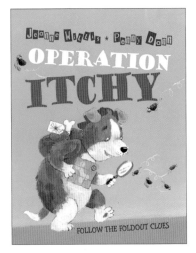

978-0-7445-9229-0

Also by Jan Fearnley

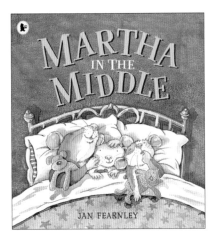

978-1-4063-1953-8

978-1-4063-0601-9

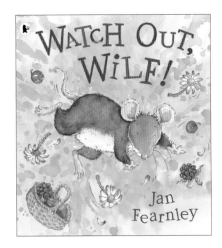

978-1-84428-509-9

Available from all good bookstores

www.walker.co.uk